Breaking Wind

Kites, Naan Bread, and Friendship

Aiden,

Read and Soar to new Heights.

Carol Paul

FERNE PRESS

Written by Carol Paul
Illustrated by Corryn Hoen

Breaking Wind
Kites, Naan Bread, and Friendship

Copyright © 2015 by Carol Paul
Layout and cover design by Jacqueline L. Challiss Hill
Cover photo by Jessica Matt
Illustrations by Corryn Hoen
Illustrations created digitally in Photoshop
Printed in the United States of America

Summary: When a new family moves in next door, Brandon has no idea how much his life will change.

Library of Congress Cataloging-in-Publication Data
    Paul, Carol
    Breaking Wind/Carol Paul–First Edition
    ISBN-13: 978-1-938326-38-7
    1. Juvenile fiction. 2. Diversity. 3. Acceptance. 4. Kite flying.
    5. Middle school.
    I. Paul, Carol II. Title
    Library of Congress Control Number: 2014953857
    Prism Hypnotist Stunt Kite is a product of Prisms Design, Inc.
    SeaWorld® and Shamu are registered trademarks of SeaWorld Parks
    & Entertainment, Inc.

FERNE PRESS

Ferne Press is an imprint of Nelson Publishing & Marketing
366 Welch Road, Northville, MI 48167
www.nelsonpublishingandmarketing.com
(248) 735-0418

Dedication

This book is dedicated to:

- Brandon Paul, my son, the most interesting main character I had the pleasure to not invent.
- Melody Paul, my daughter, the most creative person I know.
- Andrea Melton, my cousin, the inspiration for this piece of writing.
- My parents, Roy and Cheryl Melton, for allowing me to dream big.
- My Uncle Roger and Aunt Linda, who cheer me on!
- My husband, Jeremy Paul, who supports all of my crazy ideas.

I would like to acknowledge Adam Brown, a local writer, for his military service, for his appreciation for diversity, and for naan bread. Without bread, this book would have been missing an important link; thank you.

Thank you to my editor, Kris Yankee, for her hard work and dedication to this project. Also, thank you to Marian Nelson for taking a risk on a teacher from Flat Rock.

Last, I would like to recognize Pallavi Patel for sharing her books, background, and time with me. I am forever grateful and humbled by her vast knowledge and cultural awareness.

Chapter 1

Come Out, Come Out, Wherever You Are!

-Current Time-

Brandon called, "Olly, olly oxen free," as he looked through the house for his daughter. "Moti, it's past your bedtime!"

It had been thirty minutes since she had asked to play hide-and-seek. He had already looked in many different hiding places without so much as a clue to where she hid. Brandon was a master tracker. While most parents dashed around the house haphazardly hoping to catch a break, he had a system. Brandon had categorized hiding spots in ascending levels. Spots ranged from Obvious to Clever to You've Got Nerve, Kid. Now that the Obvious and Clever spaces had been scratched from the list, he was getting nervous. You've Got Nerve, Kid made him uneasy, as he began looking in bizarre areas, such as the tiny space under the bathroom sink. He opened the vanity door only to expose surplus supplies—shampoo, conditioner, shaving cream, and toilet paper. *Crash!* A noise from the laundry room drew his attention.

"I've found you!" Brandon shouted, as he walked toward the sound.

The door to the laundry room had been opened a crack. He pushed on the door only to be met with resistance. The amount of dirty laundry would not allow entry. He pushed harder, determined not to let the laundry win. The washing fought back, so Brandon pressed with gusto. Unexpectedly, the laundry surrendered and he tumbled into the room like Godzilla, stomping on the pushy clothes. As an act of revenge, a hoodie grabbed his shoe and he fell against the dryer.

"OOFF!"

The dryer slid backward and something black came clawing its way from behind.

"Hissss!"

"Aaaauuugh!" Brandon screamed in surprise.

Daisy, the family cat, flew through the air with her paws, searching for something stable to clutch onto. The cat landed on Brandon. Her claws dug into the sides of his head. Brandon began thrashing around, struggling to get the scaredy-cat off. Bottles of detergent, hangers, and spot remover fell from bumped shelves. Finally he grabbed hold of the cat's front paws and began to peel the furry critter from his face. After all claws had been removed, the cat dropped to the floor and glared at Brandon.

"Oh, don't give me that look," Brandon said to Daisy, while rubbing his wounds. "Help me look for Moti."

As he left the laundry room, Daisy trailed behind.

"Let's look in the kitchen," Brandon said to his furry companion.

They walked in and Brandon began opening every drawer. He opened the pantry and then crouched down to further investigate each shelf. Lowering himself to the tile, he moved a bag of potatoes to get a better look at the back of the pantry. Daisy rubbed up against Brandon.

"Where could she be?" Brandon asked the cat. Daisy walked to the back door.

"Oh, no. I hope Moti didn't go outside," Brandon worried.

He followed Daisy's lead and walked to the back door. Brandon checked the integrity of the door, only to discover that it was safely locked.

"Meow," Daisy whined.

"Do you want to go outside?" Brandon asked.

Daisy twisted between his calves. "Meow."

Brandon opened the door just a crack. The cool fall breeze hit his face as the cat slithered through the small opening. He closed the door and Daisy flicked her tail as if she were waving goodbye. Brandon was worried; his daughter seemed to have disappeared.

"Well, she's not in here," he said to himself. "Maybe she's hiding in one of the bedrooms."

Brandon closed and locked the back door quickly and made his way through the kitchen. He walked down the hallway, stopping at each door to listen for Moti. Finally there was a break in the case; Brandon heard soft singing coming from his own room. He whipped open the door playfully.

"Aha!" Brandon declared. "I've found you!"

He scanned the room from the doorway but did not see Moti. Then he heard the familiar singing coming from his wife's large closet. Brandon made his way to the closet. There, he found his daughter sitting on the floor digging through an old jewelry box. Her pirate hands rummaged through the box, hungry to find buried treasure.

"I found Mom's special chest," Moti said without looking up.

"Our game of hide-and-worry is over," replied Brandon. "I've been looking for over thirty minutes for you." He sat down next to Moti.

"Sorry, Daddy," Moti replied, as she continued to dig in the box.

"What are you looking for?" Brandon asked.

The little girl looked up at her father and gave a cute smile. Her attention moved back to the box.

Brandon moved closer to the little sneak. "Take it easy. I don't want you to break any of Mom's things."

"Here it is!" she exclaimed.

Moti lifted a gold necklace with a pearl pendant from the jewelry box. She let the pearl sway and spin in the air.

"Where did this come from, Daddy?"

Brandon looked at the dangling pearl and tilted his head, deep in thought.

"I gave it to your mother a long time ago," he replied.

Opening his hand, Brandon gestured for Moti to place the delicate treasure there. Her eyebrows crinkled and she pulled the necklace toward herself. Brandon waited patiently for the deposit to be made. Moti gave up and placed the necklace in her father's hand.

"I think it's beautiful," said Moti, looking up at her father with big, brown, doll-like eyes.

"Why," asked Brandon, gently folding his fingers over the pearl, "do you think it is beautiful?"

Moti drew her father's fist close to her. She softly unfolded each finger to reveal the tiny pearl. Poking at the pearl, Moti said, "It looks pretty on Mommy."

He smiled at his daughter and asked, "Do you know

the meaning of your name?"

"Please, tell me," she begged.

"Moti means pearl in Hindi," he replied. "Pearls are nature's most beautiful creations and so are you."

Moti smiled. Brandon scooped his daughter up from the floor. "It's now time, my dear, to get ready for bed."

Brandon tickled his daughter and she twisted in his arms while laughing. Moti wrapped her arms around his neck. "Tell me the story of how you met Mommy."

Thoughtfully, Brandon walked through the bedroom, taking care not to drop his precious package. He arrived at the bathroom door and gently set Moti down. The pearl necklace was still in his hand, so he fumbled with the door handle.

"I will tell you the story, but only after you have brushed your teeth." Brandon heard the cat meow at the back door. "I'm going to let in Daisy while you get to brushing."

As he walked away, he added, "Make sure you use toothpaste."

When he arrived at the back door, Daisy meowed loudly, desperate to get out of the cold. Brandon unlatched the lock and opened the door a crack. The cat slithered in, happy to be warm again. A new game, follow the leader, began as Daisy bounded toward Moti's room. Quickly closing and locking the door, Brandon followed in Daisy's pawmarks.

Daisy reached Moti's room and skillfully jumped

on the bed. Next, she began her nightly ritual: sniff the bedspread, circle the spot in question, claw the covers, and repeat. Finally a suitable cat nest had been formed and the fussy feline settled. Just as Daisy began to doze, Moti whizzed by Brandon and jumped on the bed. The startled cat let out an anxious "Meow!" and darted out of the room.

The little girl bounced under the covers while her father turned off the lamps. When touched by darkness, Moti's nightlight flickered on and gave a soft glow. Everything seemed to slow down.

Moti smoothed her covers and fluffed her pillow. "Okay, I'm ready to hear the story of how you and Mommy met."

Brandon sat at the end of his daughter's bed and began his tale of how he met her mother when he was young.

Chapter 2

Wishes Are Kooky

My mom opened the sliding back door and poked her head around the corner. "Brandon, come outside! We have a surprise for you."

As soon as I stepped onto the back porch, I heard loud singing of "Happy Birthday".

Grinning from ear to ear, I walked over to the lit cake, leaned forward, puckered my lips, and pushed a gust of wind from my lungs. *Whoosh.* The thirteen candles flickered out.

"Make a wish! Make a wish," my mother urged me. We believed in that kooky stuff, so I closed my eyes. Wish making was serious business.

In my head I said, *I wish, I wish with all my might*

that I shall get a beautiful sight. I felt hot breath on my face. I opened my eyes only to be staring at my best friend.

"What did you wish for, buddy?" De'John asked.

I pushed De'John away, playfully. "I can't tell you or it won't come true."

"Who wants cake?" my mom asked.

Hopping around like a frog, my sister shouted, "Me, me, me! Please!"

My dad leaned forward in his chair with a large box. "Here, Brandon, I hope you like it."

"Thanks, Dad," I said, as I took the rectangular box.

We had a few birthday traditions that might be considered unusual. One tradition was wrapping all presents using the Sunday comics section and the other was opening gifts with gusto. My dad had wrapped it using the Sunday comics section, so all I needed to do was make a huge fuss about opening the present.

"Ready?" my mom asked me. "One, two, three… go!"

I ripped the paper like a hungry tiger. The paper shredded and everyone clapped.

"Wow, thanks for the bow and arrow," I said, as shreds of paper floated to the ground.

"Me next, me next," chanted my four-year-old sister. "One, two, three…go!" Again I shredded the paper and found a painted rock. I was impressed by her artwork.

I admired the rainbow. "Hey, pretty cool rainbow. Thanks, Sis."

Next, De'John came over and handed me his present. "Man, I know you're going to like this." He grinned widely, showing me all of his teeth.

"One, two, three...open!" my little sister yelled. "One, two, three...open!"

As I began ripping the paper, I noticed a rainbow of colors, triangle shapes, and tails displayed on the front of the box. The more I ripped, the happier I became.

"No way!" I screamed, as I leaped into the air, shaking the package above my head. "A Prism Hypnotist Stunt Kite. Seriously?" De'John knew how much I had wanted this stunt kite. Now we could fly stunt kites together.

My buddy De'John and I had met at Willow Run Airport. Two days a month, the airport allowed stunt flyers to use the open space to practice. De'John was really smart and could perform a lot of kite stunts. He liked anything that soared—airplanes, jets, kites, rockets, spaceships, and helicopters. When my buddy daydreamed, it was usually about becoming an astronaut. Me, I didn't want to sail past the stars; instead, I wanted to design a computer program that controlled the entire space shuttle safely from the ground. Last year in seventh grade, De'John built a rocket and I made a program to tell it when to blast off.

Gently, I took the kite pieces out of the box and

spread them out on the table. I had an upper spreader, bridle, spine, connectors, lower spreader, and much more. "This may be harder to put together than I thought," I told De'John.

"I don't see why," he replied, taking hold of the spine. "I'm sure we can figure it out."

Rummaging through the box, De'John found a diagram of the kite. He studied it for a few seconds and then shoved it back in the box. "I got this," he said in an assuring tone.

After fifteen minutes, De'John picked the kite up by its spine. It twitched as the wind slapped its wings.

"This is awesome," I said, while admiring the sails. The wings were a rainbow of colors: red, green, blue, indigo, and violet. It was shaped aerodynamically just like a bird. I had been given my birthday wish.

"Do you want to put 'er up?" De'John asked.

"Yeah, but the kite could be caught in these wires or in that tree or the string might break," I replied, hugging my new kite.

"All right, so you plan to just admire the kite then?" De'John laughed.

I did want to see it fly, but I was worried. "Okay, let's go out back where there are less trees and no wires." I gave De'John a friendly punch in the arm and began to run.

"What?" De'John rubbed his wound. "Yeah, you better run," he said and started to chase after me.

I turned back around and yelled, "Thanks, Mom and

Dad!" then I rocketed toward the back with De'John trying to catch me.

The backyard was long and narrow. Trees were sparse and wires were absent. It was the perfect place to fly a kite. The wind whipped my hair around. I pushed an annoying strand from my eye. My mother always pestered me to get my hair cut.

De'John said, "Put her up."

With my arm extended and kite in hand, I began to run. May was a windy month in Michigan, and soon I felt the kite slip from my fingers. The Prism Hypnotist Stunt Kite danced in the air. One of the harder tricks I could do was a Lazy Susan. Getting into position, I pulled the strings so the kite would stop in midair and twirl.

"Score," I said. "That was awesome!"

De'John was leaning against the fence with his mouth open and his eyes to the sky. "Nice," he said. "Try a Half Axel, just like I showed you."

Hmm, Half Axel, how does that go? I thought to myself. *Oh yeah, the kite has to reverse midflight!*

I leveled the kite and allowed the wind to push it forward going west. Next, I pulled the left string to make the kite fall belly side up and then rotate. Last, I took charge and made it fly east.

"Hey, did you see that clean half-turn?" I asked De'John.

"Nice exit and good lines," he replied.

"All right," I yelled, "I'm going to try a Yo-Fade."

This jolted De'John out of his hypnotic trance. "No," he shouted. "Do not attempt a level-four trick."

I knew that the wind was right, and I felt confident that it was going to work. Again I danced with the kite, manipulated the strings, and watched the nose tilt upward. I was ready to complete the first rotation when all of a sudden the wind changed and the kite spun out of control. Everything was happening so fast. I yanked hard and my kite twisted in on itself. The string was now wrapped around one wing, which caused the kite to twirl. De'John came running toward me.

"Dude, don't let go!" he yelled.

I let go of the strings and the kite crashed in the yard next door.

De'John was out of breath. "Why...did...you...let...go?"

"You said to let go," I replied.

De'John rubbed his temples; these were his stress buttons. "I said to NOT let go."

"Oh," was all I could mutter, as I stood there looking at my wounded kite in the yard next door. There was only a chain-link fence that separated us. Walking over to the fence, I said, "The house next door is vacant." I jammed my shoe into one of the links. "I'll just jump the fence and have my kite back in no time."

As I swung my dangling leg over the fence, I heard a squeaky door open and someone started to shout. I looked around and found the source of the noise. A guy was on the back porch of the not-so-vacant house, waving his arms and speaking a language I didn't know. I hopped off the fence and the man stopped waving. He shook his head back and forth. I knew that look because my mom gave it to me when I broke her new lamp. The man turned on his heels, opened his back door, and let it slam shut. I walked back to De'John.

"Big problem, buddy," I said. "I have new neighbors and they caught me jumping the fence."

"We've got to get that kite back. Come on," De'John replied, as he marched toward the house. When we were closer to the front yard, I heard a loud crash and someone shout. De'John and I ducked behind a bush that separated the lawns. I moved a few branches carefully to keep myself hidden.

"What are they saying?" I asked.

"I don't know," he replied. "Sounds like your new neighbors don't speak English. If we asked for the kite back, they might not understand us." De'John moved a branch back so he could see the action.

"Yeah, not to mention that I have already made someone mad by climbing the fence," I replied.

I saw the back of a moving truck and a large ramp. The movers unloaded bulky boxes.

"Don't drop this box," a mover warned, "like you did the last one, Jim."

"Yeah, okay, Boss," replied the clumsy mover. Bending down, he began stacking boxes one on top of the other. After Jim had created a three-box tower, he stooped and attempted to lift all three.

The mover staggered under the weight. "Whoa!" He steadied himself and began to walk across the lawn with a structure that resembled the Leaning Tower of Pisa. His cheek was smashed up against the back of the second box, which obviously made it hard to see the impending doom that lay ahead—a ball, mole hill, and tricycle.

"Oh, man, he's a goner," I noted.

De'John and I continued to hold our breath as Jim approached his first obstacle: the ball.

Will he make it? I wondered.

The mover was right up on the ball and accidently kicked it. "Sorry," he said to his victim. Just a few steps further and he would encounter the mole hill. One step. Two steps. Three steps.

"I can't look." De'John covered his eyes just as the mover stepped directly into the hill. The ground swelled up and sucked his shoe right off his foot.

"Ahhhhh!" he yelled and twirled with the stacked boxes. "What happened to my shoe?"

All the whirling and twirling created an unbalanced tower and he stumbled backward. The third hurdle, a tricycle, was right behind Jim.

"Come on, let's help him," De'John whispered. We popped up out of our viewing spot. The tower began to crumble just as De'John and I arrived. I grabbed the first falling box and De'John the other.

"Wow, thanks, guys," Jim said, as he stood there with one shoe on and a brow full of sweat. "You saved my job. Say, how's about keeping this between you and me?"

"Sure," De'John replied.

"So, are you new here?" Jim asked.

De'John and I looked at each other. Sure, we were both tall and I supposed we could look like we were old enough for a job. "Yeah, sure. Where should we take these boxes?"

"Set 'em in the kitchen," Jim replied.

De'John and I slowly walked toward the house, grinning broadly. A new unspoken plan had just developed.

The porch was narrow, railed, and spanned the length of the house. The white rails allowed one person to enter or exit. The porch was busy with movers hustling to grab the next box. I waited my turn patiently and then gingerly placed my foot on the porch.

I heard someone say, "Hold the door," from inside the house. The screen door flung open and I jumped out of the way just in time. Two large men came out of the house, hauling a weird concrete figurine.

"She wants this out back," one burly man said.

"Brandon, let's follow them," De'John said.

Jumping off the porch, I followed De'John and the movers to the backyard.

"There it is, smack dab in the middle of the yard," I whispered to De'John. He nodded.

The movers kept walking, but we stopped.

I said, "I'm gonna grab the kite and then we can run out of here."

As I darted for the kite, box still in hand, I heard the familiar squeaky sound of the back door opening behind me.

Oh no! I thought. *I've been caught.* I froze. *If I don't move, they won't see me.*

"No, that box goes to the kitchen," said a girlish voice.

I had been spotted. Relaxing my petrified state, I turned around only to find the most fascinating girl I had ever seen. Her skin was a caramel color, her long dark hair was braided, and she had on the most colorful clothes. My mouth dropped and so did the box. The words "most beautiful sight" popped into my head. I walked across the lawn stupefied, but the girl grabbed a watering can and went into the house.

"Brandon," I heard De'John say, "grab the kite."

I had totally forgotten about the kite.

"Never mind. I'll do it myself." De'John set his box down on the grass and walked past me. He grabbed the kite and then my shirt. "Come on, let's go."

I had squandered my chance to meet the captivating girl who lived next door, but there was always tomorrow.

Chapter 3

Pain in the Neck

I woke up early the next morning and stayed in bed for a while. Saturday mornings were relaxed at my house. I heard little footsteps coming toward my bedroom. I knew it was my sister, so I rolled over and pretended to be asleep. As I had expected, Melody gave a quick knock on my door and then flung it open.

"Brando Commando!" she called. Melody calls me funny rhyming names like Brandon Fandon, Tandon, or Glandon. She is really amazing with words for being so little.

I snored loudly but kept my eyes shut. I could hear the pint-sized sneak shuffling along the hardwood floor. "Brandon," she whispered, "are you still sleeping?"

Keeping my back to her, I replied with another loud snore. I felt her little hands grab the covers. The blanket began sliding off of my shoulders as she pulled it to the floor. Soon I was coverless and Melody was shaking my arm.

"Wake up!" she said.

I rolled over quickly and snatched her up in my arms. She began to squeal.

"I've got you, my pretty!" I cackled like the Wicked Witch of the West from Oz and began to tickle her ribs.

She laughed so hard, I heard a snort. I stopped tickling so she could take a breath.

"I knew you were faking," she said.

"Oh, really?" I replied and began tickling her again. This time Melody wiggled her way out of my arms and dashed across the room.

"Mom made pancakes," she yelled, as she jetted down the stairs.

"In that case, I won't hurry," I shouted from my bed.

As I walked across my bedroom to shut the door, something caught my eye. It was the broken birthday kite. My stomach flipped, not because of the fractured wing but because it reminded me of the girl next door. In my mind, I began to draw a silhouette of her face. Her skin was painted caramel and her eyes a chocolate brown. Trying to get the still-life out of my brain, I shook my head like a wet dog. As I stood there dizzy, the image disappeared.

I found an old T-shirt in my closet and a pair of jeans. I pulled the shirt over my head and then slipped out of my pajama bottoms. The pj's were replaced by ripped jeans. I glanced at myself in the mirror that hung on the door. My reflection had messy hair. I was considered skinny, yet tall for my age. Grandma Melton was always asking, "Can I get you a cookie?" This was her polite way of telling me to put some meat on my bones.

I leaned closer to my carbon copy and asked, "What you lookin' at?"

I stepped back and assumed the "Crane" stance from *The Karate Kid.* With one leg up and wings in the air, I delivered a deadly kick to my duplicate. "Gotcha!" I shouted and yanked the door open, a satisfied victor.

My bedroom door's golden handle caught my eye and I remembered the short necklace that wrapped gently around my neighbor's neck. The necklace had a small round charm attached. As if I had water in my ear, I tilted my egghead to one side and began shaking. My brain held the mental photograph tight and would not let it go. I jumped up and down with my neck craned to one side. No luck, the thought was stuck. Thankfully my mother called from the kitchen, "Brandon, pancakes are ready," and the image flew out of my head.

"Coming, just need to brush my teeth."

Stop thinking about her, I thought to myself while walking into the bathroom. I grabbed the toothpaste and toothbrush and worked really hard to focus on the task at hand. As I washed my face and combed my hair, a new image lingered. A soft wind was unfolding her braid and long strands of black hair were gently swaying in the breeze. I stopped brushing and gave my head another good wobble. This time the jostling was enough to wake me up. *I've got to get out of here*, I thought and bolted downstairs to the kitchen.

"Whoa, you look like you've just seen a ghost," my mom said, as I walked in the kitchen. "Are you feeling all right?"

"I'm just tired," I replied.

"Well, grab a plate," she said.

"Can I just have juice?"

"Sure, go ahead," she replied.

I opened the cabinet door and took out a small glass.

"So, what are you doing today?" Mom asked, while flipping a pancake.

"I don't know. I think I'm gonna just mess around."

"Well, can you take out the trash before you begin such important work?" she inquired with a smile.

I opened the refrigerator and hunted for the juice. The jug was nowhere to be found.

"Sure, I can take out the trash," I said, closing the fridge. "Do you know where the juice is hiding?"

"Yep, on the table." Mom flicked her spatula in the direction of the kitchen table.

I filled my glass and walked outside to the back

porch. My mom was great at many things, but cooking was not one of them. As I slid the door shut, I heard her saying to Mel, "Take from this stack; it's not burnt."

I navigated my way through the jungle of potted plants to a folding chair. I plopped down and the rickety chair protested with a loud creak. The orange juice was cold and the glass was perspiring in my hand. It was unusually warm and dry for the month of May. I leaned my head back and closed my eyes. Again I thought of the girl on the porch. *What in the world is wrong with me? Why can't I get her out of my head?* I began to jangle my head around again. *Well, I can't keep doing this. I am going to look awfully silly jumping around trying to get my head straight.*

Just then my super sniffer took over. I knew the fresh smell was not coming from our kitchen. "What is that wonderful smell?" I asked myself, inhaling deeply. Delicious fumes were wafting from the house next door. I got up from the chair and went to the shared fence. Leaning toward the smell, I closed my eyes and sucked in the aroma. I heard someone giggle. Startled, I opened my eyes to see the beautiful girl.

"What are you doing?" she asked.

"Smelling something amazing," I replied.

"What you're smelling is *naan* bread," the girl said quietly.

"Which is...?" I prompted.

"It's a flat bread that my mother and I make together every day. Would you like to try some?"

The girl tore a piece of bread and handed it to me. I took the bread and popped it into my mouth. "Tasty," I mumbled with a mouthful of food. I chewed slowly, loving each and every bite.

"Wow, you really like *naan* bread," the girl observed. "What's your name?"

I swallowed the flat bread. "Brandon," I responded. "What's yours?"

"My name is Pallavi."

"So, I am starting to think you're pretty far from home." I clamped my lips shut. I felt really stupid for making assumptions and then actually saying them aloud. After that first-class move, I was suddenly very interested in a small anthill. I used my shoe to upset the colony. Ants were spreading like wildfire.

"What makes you think that?" she teased. "Might it be my delicious bread?"

I smiled and shrugged, relieved that she didn't find me rude. "Well, yesterday I heard someone at your house speaking another language, your clothes are not like mine, and this bread is unlike anything I have ever tasted, so maybe another country?" The swarms of butterflies in my stomach were now performing daredevil acts. Tension and excessive sweating were making it difficult to act cool.

"I'm from India, specifically Vadodara in Gujarat," Pallavi replied.

"You are far from home," I responded. "So, what's Vadodara like?"

"Well, the city streets are crowded, but people are friendly and kind. The uptown shopping areas have small stores where you can buy fruits, grains, vegetables, thread, and saris. We moved to the United States because my father received a job at the University of Michigan," Pallavi said.

Just then I heard someone say loudly, "Pallavi, get away from the fence!"

"Coming, *Pitaji*," Pallavi called over her shoulder. "My father is calling me. *Namaste.*"

"Wait, don't go," I said with a hint of desperation in my voice. "We were just getting to know each other."

"Maybe another day I can show you how to make *naan* bread." She gave a small wave and walked away from the fence.

"Tomorrow!" I squeaked and turned to leave. "In the meantime, I hope to get you out of my head," I mumbled to myself. Walking back to the porch, my neck began to ache. "Also, I might need a few aspirin."

Chapter 4

This Puppy Is
Barking Up the Wrong Tree

The next day, I saw De'John ride up the driveway on his bike.

"Mom, I'm going to Hobby Hill with De'John!" I yelled.

She popped her head out of her bedroom. "Be careful and stay on the sidewalk. It's always busy downtown on Sundays," she warned.

"Sure thing," I replied.

I opened the front door and walked over to the garage.

De'John rode over to me. "We have to get your kite flying for next weekend's tournament," he said. "I have a list of supplies that we can use to repair it." He shoved the list in my face.

"Just let me get my bike out of the garage," I replied, while bending down to lift the garage door handle. I had to pull with all my strength to get that old door open. It lifted in one massive piece to reveal holiday decorations and some tools. I moved a large plastic pumpkin to get to my bike. After walking out of the garage, I dropped my bike in the grass.

"Something weird happened to me yesterday," I said, while closing the door.

"Did your mom cook an amazing meal?" De'John chuckled at his own joke.

"No, seriously," I replied. "Listen, I know this is strange, but I can't stop thinking about the girl next door."

De'John was quiet for a moment and then he got a huge grin on his face. "Sounds like puppy love to me."

"Yuck!" I yelled and made a sick face.

"Well, sounds like it to me anyway." De'John laughed. He was enjoying my misery. "Here, take the list, puppy love!" he poked again. This time I snatched the list from him and began inspecting the items. He added, "I had to substitute some stuff, because Hobby Hill doesn't have it."

I slid the list into my back pocket, grateful he had dropped the whole puppy love thing. "Well, let's hope this works," I said. "That tournament next week decides who will move on to nationals."

"Okay, let's get going," De'John replied, while

swinging his bike around toward the sidewalk. I picked my bike up from the grass and followed behind.

We arrived at Hobby Hill about twenty minutes later. My mom was right; everyone from town was down here shopping. De'John and I rode our bikes up to the front of the store where we could stow them.

"Man, this place is crowded," De'John noted. I nodded in agreement. "Let's grab the stuff we need and get out of here."

We walked through the huge doors and weaved our way over to the doweled rods. The brace of the kite was broken from the fall. We knew that a fiberglass rod was best but impossible to find at Hobby Hill. "Where's the list?" De'John asked. "What size rod do we need?"

I slid the slip of paper from my back pocket and referred to the list. I went over to the bin and began digging. "We need one-fourth diameter," I replied.

De'John dug through the bin. "I got it!" he said, while pulling the rod from the box. He shot the rod into the air as if it were an unsheathed sword. "En guard!" De'John barked, as he lowered the dowel and began poking an imaginary opponent.

"All right, King Arthur, we have to get thread, fabric, and

~ 33 ~

material," I teased. De'John stopped in his tracks.

"Wow, we really need a new hobby," he said, as he lowered his sword. "Right now, I feel like we should join my grandma's quilting bee." His imaginary sword became a huge needle as he pretended to sew.

Mimicking his grandma's voice, I said, "Now, Sonny, careful with that needle."

"Not cool, dude," De'John replied with a serious look on his face. "Grammy Lee doesn't sound like that."

"Oh, sorry," I immediately regretted the bad impression I had done of Grammy Lee.

"Just kidding, Sonny!" De'John said in his best Grammy Lee voice.

"Oh, man, I thought you were serious!" I smiled.

In his deepest, manliest voice, De'John said, "Okay, now off to buy some needles and thread."

We both laughed hysterically and walked to aisle ten.

There were so many different kinds of fabric, thread, and needles. We went to the fabric first. We began touching all the fabrics looking for something similar to the original sail.

"Too rough," I said.

"Too soft," De'John said.

"Too stiff. We'll never find fabric like polyethylene," I whined. "Goldilocks had more success than us!"

"Don't worry, dude, we'll find something," De'John said. "Maybe we're looking in the wrong department. I have an idea. Grab those needles and some thread." He motioned to the shelf. "And let's go to the tent section."

I grabbed a small packet of needles, some white thread, and followed De'John to the camping aisle.

"Look, we can buy one of these children's tents," De'John said, "and then cut it up to use for your sail."

"Well, hello boys," said a familiar voice. I looked over to find Principal Cole sifting through the canteens. It was weird seeing her outside school.

"Hello, Principal Cole," De'John and I said together.

"So, what are you two up to?" she asked.

"We're repairing a broken kite," I said.

"Yes, that's right! The tournament is next weekend," she replied.

My eyeballs just about popped out of my head and De'John's mouth dropped to the ground. First, what was Principal Cole doing away from school, and second, how does she know about the tournament?

I rubbed my eyes and said, "We're going to cut up this tent and use it for a sail."

"Yep, that might work and these tents are cheap," she said. "Well, you better get to work if you want to test your kite."

"Sure," I agreed.

I had a few rolls of thread and a packet of needles in my hands. The tent came in a bulky box. "Here, take this thread," I said to De'John, while I shoved the packet of needles into my back pocket. I lifted the tent box into my arms and walked toward the front of the store.

"'Bye, Principal Cole," I shouted over my shoulder.

"Good luck," she replied.

De'John and I found the shortest route to the register. My arms were beginning to ache from the weight of the bulky box. As soon as we found the shortest line, I dropped the box to the floor. The noise made the customer in front of us turn around.

"Hey, buddies!" It was Jim from the moving company. "How's it going?"

"Pretty good, thanks," De'John replied.

"Have you been on any jobs recently?" he asked.

"I think you're up," I motioned to the cashier who was waiting to ring up Jim's purchases.

"Oh," Jim turned and began unloading his cart.

De'John and I both gave each other a knowing glance. This was the guy who we sort of lied to about being movers. De'John whispered, "That cashier saved us from a tough conversation. Just act cool."

I stepped away from De'John and turned to watch Jim's transaction. He was chatting about the weather with the cashier and seemed to have forgotten about De'John and me.

Thank goodness, I thought.

As the cashier bagged up his stuff, Jim turned his attention back to us. "So, what are you guys planning, a camping trip?" He gave a sideways glance.

"No, we're trying to repair a kite," De'John answered, as he began hauling all of our items onto the conveyer belt.

"Sweet, sounds like fun," Jim said, as he picked up his bags. The cashier began ringing up our items and placing them in a bag. She struggled to find the bar code on the bulky box.

"I'm going to have to call for a price check," the cashier told us, as she picked up the phone and punched in a few numbers. "I need a price check on a purple and white girl's play tent," her voice rang over the loudspeaker.

De'John and I looked at each other in disbelief. We had picked a girl's tent! Suddenly my shoe became very interesting, while De'John began rubbing his temples. Jim had a puzzled look on his face. The cashier hung up the phone and waited for an answer.

Brrrng, Brrrng. The sound of the telephone brought everyone back to life. Our cashier answered the phone and began punching in a few numbers. She hung up the phone and said to me, "That will be eleven dollars and fifty-three cents." I handed her twelve dollars. She made change and I opened my hand to receive the coins. "Have a great day," she said, as I walked away with the bulky girl's tent in my arms.

"You, too," I replied while hurrying out of the store.

"Hey, wait!" the cashier shouted. "You have something sticking out of your back pocket."

I whipped around quickly with the tent only to bump into my new next door neighbor.

The cashier came out from behind the register

and confronted me. "You did not pay for whatever is sticking out of your back pocket."

Pallavi's father gave me a disappointed look and ushered a woman, probably his wife, around the scene. They left the store in a hurry.

"I forgot the package of needles were in my pocket," I began to explain. "The tent box was hard to manage, so I told my friend to hold the thread and I put the needles in my pocket with the list."

De'John just nodded. "Yep, that's what happened," he said.

"Boys, is everything all right?" I heard Principal Cole ask from somewhere behind me.

"No, I didn't mean to steal anything," I begged. "I just forgot about the needles."

Principal Cole said, "That's right. I was in the same aisle and saw the boys trying to lug that bulky box."

"Yes," Jim said, "these two work for my uncle's moving company and are stand-up guys!"

Principal Cole looked puzzled. "Work for a moving company?"

De'John quickly changed the subject. "We can pay for the needles. Sorry about the confusion."

"Yes, here's the money." I set the tent down and began digging through my pockets.

"All right, sounds like it was all just a big misunderstanding," the cashier replied. "Come back around and I'll ring up the needles."

"Thanks, Mrs. Cole and Jim," I said while walking

to the register.

"No problem, Mr. Movers." Mrs. Cole gave me a wink.

"Yeah, about that..." De'John began to explain.

"I'll see you boys at school," she said to De'John and walked away.

"That will be five dollars and seventy-five cents," the cashier said in a not-so-nice tone.

I gave her six bucks and waited for the quarter. She opened the register and then gave me my change. This time I did not get the cute "Have a nice day."

De'John and I rode home in silence. I had the tent balanced on my handlebars, while he had the bag hooked on his handlebar grips. As soon as we got home, Mom opened the front door and said, "De'John's mom called and wants him to come home."

"'Bye, dude," I said.

"See you tomorrow," he replied, as he placed the bag on the front lawn.

As I dumped my bike and tent in the grass, I heard *twingle-twang*. It sounded sort of like a high-pitched guitar. I looked around to find where the noise was coming from. *Twingle-twang, twingle-twang* floated through the air and hit my eardrum. It was coming from behind the house, so I walked along the driveway that led to the backyard. I looked over the fence and saw Pallavi strumming a funny-looking guitar.

"Hello!" I yelled over the music.

Pallavi stopped playing. "Oh, I hope I'm not

bothering you!" she shouted back.

"Do you know what I love about your guitar? The unique sound it makes," I said while pretending to strum an imaginary guitar.

Pallavi chuckled and walked over to the fence. "It is called a sitar. It has thirteen strings." She lifted the instrument above the fence. "This is called a *dandi*," she pointed to the neck of the sitar, "and this is the *kaddu*," she pointed to the base of the sitar. Next she sat down on the grass and crossed her legs. She propped the base of the sitar on her foot and angled the neck up toward the blue sky. "Listen closely," said Pallavi. "I am going to play a piece composed by Manju Mehta, a female sitarist." The high-pitched sounds filled the air and Pallavi's hands flew up and down the *dandi.* Pallavi stood when she was finished and asked, "Well, what did you think?"

Without hesitation, I replied, "Well, it made my day seem much better."

"Good." Pallavi smiled. "The piece was intended to brighten one's spirit."

"Pallavi, get away from that boy!" I heard someone yell.

"Sorry, I must go. My mother is calling me," she said.

"Maybe tomorrow you can show me more," I said.

"Maybe," she said, while walking toward the house.

I heard Pallavi's mother say, "Stay away from that boy. I saw him at Hobby Hill today." Pallavi's mother opened the door and the conversation became muffled.

My heart sank; her mother thought I was a bad kid. One bad impression had sealed the deal. Our puppy love was now barking up the wrong tree.

Chapter 5

Soaring Through Differences

My arms were extended wide and wind hit my face. I looked down and realized I was flying high above a large grassy area. I could see my next-door neighbor looking up at me with her arms outstretched. This was weird but cool! I felt happy and free. From the ground, Pallavi pulled back her left shoulder just as I felt something tug at my left wrist. I looked over and noticed a long string coming from my wrist to Pallavi. Her pull had caused me to change course. I felt another tug, this time on my right arm, which caused me to change course again.

Buzz.

What was that noise? I whipped my head left and

then right, trying to find the source.

Buzz.

The noise was right in front of me.

Buzz.

I looked forward only to find a giant bee the size of my head barreling down on me. Panic flooded through me and my body flailed in the air.

Buzz.

I could tell he was angry and did not want to share air space with me. Terror set in, and I began to thrash around mid-flight.

Buzz.

The animated bee tilted his abdomen toward my face and showed me his giant stinger.

Buzz.

I closed my eyes and yelled, "Get me down from here, Pallavi!"

My grounded puppet master realized I was in trouble and said, "Brandon, wake up."

I blinked my eyes open and found my mother standing over me. "Brandon, wake up. I turned off your alarm. It had been going off for a few minutes," she said.

I sat up and rubbed my chest. I could feel my heart beating fast. "Wow, I had the worst dream."

"I could tell," she said. "You were whipping around."

"I was an out-of-control kite," I said, as I checked my wrists for remnants of string.

"Sounds to me like you're spending too much time thinking about that tournament," she said, while leaning in to ruffle my hair.

"Maybe," I replied.

My mom's high heels clicked on the hardwood floor as she walked toward the bedroom door. "I have to get going or I'm going to be late for work. Do you need me to pack a lunch for you?" she asked over her shoulder.

"Nope," I replied.

"Okay, have a good day, and don't be late for the bus." She shut the door behind her.

I turned and looked at the clock.

"Seven forty-five!" I screamed.

The next fifteen minutes were a blur of clothes, face, teeth, lunch, shoes, and backpack. Hearing the screeching bus brakes, I flew down the driveway and leaped onto the bus just in time! I found the first empty seat and plopped down. I hunched over, trying to catch my breath.

"Are you okay?" I heard someone ask from across the bus aisle.

Breathy, I replied, "Just a bad morning."

I heard the plastic bus seat crunch and then a light blue scarf slid into view. The scarf looked out of place next to the dirty floor of the bus. My eyes trailed up the fabric until they landed upon Pallavi's brown eyes. I gulped.

"I'm fine, just got up late," I said. "Today's your first day, right?"

She leaned in close to me and whispered, "Yes."

With a huge grin on my face, I whispered back, "Well, don't think no one will notice because our school is really big."

Pallavi's expression changed. She looked terrified and tried to disappear within the bus seat again.

We were both silent until the bus pulled into the middle school parking lot.

"Eek," I heard Pallavi yelp as the bus lurched into its designated spot in front of the school.

Hoping to make up for my earlier mistake, I asked, "Do you need me to show you where to get your schedule?"

Pallavi smiled politely. "Thanks."

The bus driver opened the door and everyone piled out in a single-file line. I caught up with Pallavi at the double doors leading into the school.

"This way," I motioned and she followed me down the hallway to the office.

As we walked in, Mrs. Palencar, the school counselor, greeted us. "Hello. What can I do you for?"

I replied, "This is Pallavi. She's new to our school."

The counselor said to Pallavi, "Your dad called on Friday to let us know you would be coming. Brandon, I can take it from here. Thanks."

"What lunch does Pallavi have?" I asked.

Mrs. Palencar consulted the computer. "Looks like A lunch."

Before I turned to leave, I asked, "Save you a seat at lunch?"

Pallavi nodded yes and then gave me a shy smile.

I walked out of the office. Even though it was smelly tuna casserole day in the cafeteria, I could not wait for lunch!

In my first hour, which was study hall, I tried to finish up my homework but couldn't stop thinking about lunch. In my second hour, I learned about solving for X. Again, I had trouble concentrating. In my third hour, De'John and I met up. We goofed around in gym together until Mr. Bravo said, "Boys, get your heads in the game!" Soccer was a big deal to Mr. Bravo, so we started trying to score and block. De'John made a goal, but we still didn't win.

Finally it was time for lunch, so De'John and I made our way to the cafeteria with bagged lunches.

"Let's save a seat for Pallavi," I said to De'John.

He started making kissy noises in my direction.

I rolled my eyes. "Whatever, dude."

"No, I'm just kidding," he replied. "She seems pretty cool."

I opened the door to the cafeteria and the smell slapped me in the face.

"Yuck, tuna fish casserole," De'John reported.

We clamped down on our noses and made our way past the kitchen.

I sat down at our usual table and faced the door so I could see when Pallavi came in. I was still pinching my nose.

"We can't eat without unclamping our noses," De'John said. "On the count of three, we will release." De'John started counting. "One...two..."

Just then the lunchroom door swung open and Pallavi appeared. I jumped up, forgetting about the tuna smell and started waving my arms frantically. She made an awful face and began to back out of the cafeteria. Before I knew it, she was gone.

I stopped waving and sagged back into my seat. "Well, I blew it, De'John! Pallavi came in and I started waving my arms like a baboon."

"No biggie. She'll come back around again," De'John replied.

After lunch, I had social studies, art, and English. Between classes, I looked for Pallavi, but our paths never crossed. After the last bell rang, I met De'John in the hallway.

"Do you want to come over to help me fix my kite?" I asked.

"Sure, let's walk," he replied.

We started to walk home, talking about the kite tournament and our teachers. Later we ended up in the garage with my broken kite, glue, needle, thread, and other tools to put it all back together again.

After about forty-five minutes of working, I heard the front door of Pallavi's house close.

"Hey, do you think I should go talk to Pallavi?" I asked De'John. "I kind of want to know what happened today."

"Yeah, maybe you should hang out in the backyard," he replied, while pushing a needle through the torn wing.

"No, only chickens do that. I should just walk up to the front door and ask to speak to Pallavi."

"Good luck with that," De'John said sarcastically. "Her parents seem not to like you much. Remember leaping the fence or the scene at Hobby Hill? Might not have made the best first impression. Also, you may do or say something wrong. Her family is different, I can tell." De'John made the last stitch to the wing and then the universal sign for scissors with his hands.

Giving him the scissors, I said, "Still, I want to find out what happened to her at school."

It was obvious that I had made up my mind to knock on Pallavi's front door, so De'John gave up, clipped the thread, and inspected his handiwork.

After tugging on the wing, he said, "All right, buddy, go ahead." He then threaded the needle again and began repairing the ripped tail.

It was a short walk, but I was tense. Pallavi's family was different than mine; what if I said or did something wrong again? I approached the driveway and found myself unable to move. "Come on, feet, just one foot in front of the other."

I had some trouble making it up the driveway

but eventually hopped up on the porch and knocked on Pallavi's front door. Her father answered the door.

"Is Pallavi home?" I asked.

Her father scowled. "Yes, but she may not speak to someone so disrespectful."

"I just wanted to see if she was okay," I  stammered. "I didn't see her after lunch."

"She is of no concern to you," he replied sternly.

I turned away from Pallavi's father, confused and angry. As I walked past the front window, I caught a glimpse of her blue scarf and long dark hair. I heard the front door close, and my heart broke.

My mother always told me to never cut across the grass, but I did because I was mad. I stormed into the garage and De'John stopped working. "Well, that was fast. What happened, Romeo?"

"Her father said I was disrespectful!" I shouted.

"What did you do to him?"

"Nothing. I did nothing," I replied.

"Well, you had to have done something," he said. "Folks just don't make things up."

"Nope, nothing."

My dad pulled up the driveway and parked.

He gathered his things out of the car. "Hey, boys, how are the kite repairs going?" he asked.

"The kite repairs are fine, but other things are not so good," I replied.

"What's up?" he asked.

I told him about hopping the fence, Hobby Hill, and school.

He said, "Son, stay away from those people. I knew the minute they moved in they would be different. Did you see the strange statues and furniture they were carting into that house? Also, I tried to give a friendly wave yesterday and the guy bowed. It made me feel uncomfortable, so I just walked away. Their clothes are different and the music is awful. If I were you, I would just leave that family alone."

My dad's little speech did help. I wasn't mad anymore, just sad. I liked Pallavi and thought she was interesting. Maybe if I learned more about her culture, we as a family could gain new friends. My dad gave me a friendly punch in the arm.

"Hey, don't look so down in the dumps," he said.

As he walked into the house, I said to De'John, "Let's forget the kite for a minute and learn more about our neighbors."

"Hey, that's a great attitude!" De'John put his hand in the air and said, "Up top!" I complied and gave him a high-five. We both laughed.

Chapter 6

Igniting a New Friendship

The next day, I hopped off the bus quickly to find De'John. He was standing next to his locker, shoving his backpack inside.

As I approached he asked, "Was Pallavi on the bus?"

"I looked but didn't see her," I replied.

"Well, is your master plan still to learn about her culture?" De'John asked.

"It sure is. Do you think you could meet me in the library during first hour?" I inquired.

"Mr. Sullivan is pretty cool, so I bet he'll let me," De'John replied.

"Okay. I know Mrs. Scoles will let me go. I have study hall."

I walked in to my first hour and slid into my assigned seat, waiting for Mrs. Scoles to do roll call. Right after she said Christopher Yannick's name, I shot my hand up in the air. She nodded in my direction.

"Mrs. Scoles, can I go to the library to do research?" I asked.

"Do you have a paper due in another class?" she asked.

"Yes, I have to research Gujarat for my geography class," I replied. It was not a lie; I really did have to present on a country of my choice. Originally I was going to do a paper on Japan, but now India was much more appealing.

She handed me a pass and made a shooing motion toward the door. "Now, the rest of you should take out your homework."

I walked to the library. I looked for De'John but no luck. Ms. Davis, our school librarian, was behind her desk using a scanner to check in books. She was humming and smiling as she worked. Many students called her Mary Poppins because she always saw the bright side of things. I walked up to the desk, but Ms. Davis was so into scanning and humming that she didn't notice me. I cleared my throat and leaned on her desk.

She stopped mid-scan and looked up. "Hello. How are you, Brandon?"

"Good," I replied.

"Well, how can I help you today?" Ms. Davis asked.

"I need to use a computer," I responded.

"Sure, when you log in, be certain to use your school user ID and password." She used the scanner as a pointer. "Pick any computer behind the encyclopedias."

I walked through a maze of bookshelves to get to the computers. Really, who needs books anymore? Computers are the way to go; you can always find reliable information on the web!

I logged on, just as Ms. Davis had advised, and waited for the search screen to pop up. I clicked on the browser and typed "Gujarat, Vadodara." One hundred thirty million results appeared in seven seconds. "Aghh," I groaned. Nothing was going to be fast about this search. I clicked on the first link and began scanning for anything that would help me understand Pallavi.

"Looks like a lot of reading, Brandon," De'John said from behind me.

I turned around. "I see Mr. Sullivan let you out."

De'John flashed his hall pass. "Maybe a good old-fashioned book would be better," he suggested.

"No, just give me a sec." I turned and looked at the computer screen. "It says here that the British once called Vadodara 'Baroda' so they could easily pronounce the city's name. It regained its native name after the British left."

"Well, that's a good start."

"This site also says that several languages are spoken."

"Like what, Hindi?"

"Yes, Hindi is the official language of India, but Gujarati is the language most spoken in Gujarat, Vadodara."

"Wow, do you think Pallavi can speak Hindi?" De'John asked.

"Maybe," I replied. "Hey, this is cool. MSU is located in Gujarat."

"What would Michigan State University be doing in Gujarat?" De'John asked.

"No, it is called Maharaja Sayajirao University of Baroda," I corrected. "There are over thirty thousand students at this one university."

"Do you think Pallavi's father worked at Maharaja Sayajirao University?"

"I don't know, but it might be a good conversation to have with Pallavi's dad," I said.

"Maybe we should check out a few books." De'John moved away from the computer and began poking around the books.

I logged off and rolled the chair away from the desk. "Let's ask Ms. Davis."

De'John led the way back through the maze of books toward the front of the library.

"Wow! That was fast," Ms. Davis noted, as we approached.

"We decided it would be best if I checked out books to take home," I said.

"Well, what are you looking for?" she asked.

Hopeful, I asked, "I want to learn about India. Do you have any books on that?"

Ms. Davis began banging on her keyboard. She leaned toward the computer screen and made noises like *hmm* and *umm*. After the computer consult was over, she looked up at us with a huge grin and said, "I've got it!"

She wrote down a few numbers on a piece of paper. Coming from behind the desk, Ms. Davis went directly to a long row of shelves. She placed her finger on the binding of the books and kept referencing the numbers on the piece of paper.

"Here we go!" she said with delight. Ms. Davis began hauling books from the shelf, passing them to me, and reading titles aloud, "*National Geographic Traveler, Planes, Trains, and Auto-rickshaws, India-Culture Smart*, and *The Rough Guide to India*."

When my arms were full, Ms. Davis walked back toward the desk. "Let's get you checked out."

I put the books on her desk and gave her my school library card. Ms. Davis scanned the card and the books. With a satisfied grin, she slid the pile of books to me. "It was a pleasure book hunting with you, Brandon."

"Thanks, Ms. Davis, for your help," I said happily.

In the hallway, De'John jokingly said, "Looks like you have some major reading to do!"

"Oh, I don't want you to worry," I said in a smart-aleck tone. "You get to read a few of these yourself."

De'John gave a sly sideways smile. "Nice try. If

anyone needs me, I'll be in class." He bolted, leaving me with the heavy load of books.

That day, I read every chance I got. If a teacher gave a few minutes of free time to talk, I was reading. At lunch, I brought a book and read while eating. In sixth hour, I sneaked it and read under my desk while others were reciting their poems in front of the class. I even read on the bus. I continued to read while walking up my driveway.

"Hey, bookworm, can I get your help?" someone asked.

I looked up from the *National Geographic Traveler* to find my father.

"Oh, sure."

"You should probably go inside, drop your books, and get changed," he suggested. "We're going to be working in the garden, and it's a hot one today."

Inside, I tossed my books on the kitchen table. I ran up to my room, put on some shorts, and met my dad by the garden.

"Brandon, can you go to the shed and grab a shovel while I pull weeds?" he asked.

"Sure thing," I said, while heading toward the shed. I opened the latch that held the door and it swung open.

"Aw, the shovel is in the back," I whined.

I made my way toward the back of the dark shed. "Ouch!"

I had bumped my head against a large shelf and

there was an avalanche.

Rubbing the fresh bump beginning to form on my head, I thought, *Great, now I have to clean up this mess.*

I kicked a few cans out of the way and walked much more cautiously. A few steps later, I robbed the corner of its shovel and headed out the door.

"Brandon! Do you have the shovel?" my dad yelled from the garden.

"Yep!" I yelled back. While walking back to Dad, I noticed Pallavi and her father in their backyard. I waved at Pallavi and she gave a secret wave back.

"Which plants are you digging up?" I asked my dad, who was busy pulling weeds. He pointed to the grape hyacinth.

I pierced the dirt with my shovel and used my foot to push its nose under the plant. Careful not to damage any roots, I pushed down on the handle and the plant gently gave up its hold. Grabbing the base of the leaves, I tossed it in the wheelbarrow. The noise startled my dad and he looked up.

He wiped his forehead and said, "First plant out, nice work."

"Do you want all these out?" I pointed.

"Yes, they are taking over the garden," he confirmed.

I turned and poked around the base of my next plant.

"*Aag! Aag!* Fire! Fire!"

I turned to see Pallavi's father pointing at our shed. Smoke was seeping from a small vent in the roof and flames were visible by the door. My dad and I zipped to the house. I turned the water spigot to the right while Dad ran with the hose. He sprayed the front of the shed full force, but it was not enough. I could now see the fire begin to lick the sides of the shed.

Pallavi's father yelled to his daughter. "Turn on the water! They need help!"

He grabbed his hose, ran across the yard, and shot the shed with a blast of water. Soon the flames flickered out. No one had been hurt. Dad reached over the picket fence and offered a handshake to Pallavi's father.

The men shook hands, and my father said, "Thank you, neighbor."

Pallavi's father pressed his palms together, fixed his fingers below his chin, nodded his head, and said "Namaste, neighbor. I bow to you out of respect."

My father pressed his palms together, fixed his fingers below his chin, nodded his head, and said, "Namaste. I bow to you out of respect."

My dad turned to me and I looked up at him. "What happened in the shed that would cause a fire?" he asked.

I stared up into his eyes. "I knocked over a few cans."

My dad was a no-nonsense kind of guy, but he cared about me. "The liquid must have mixed like a chemistry experiment. Those chemicals started the fire," he said. "I'm glad no one was hurt." He gave me a hug.

I whispered, "Sorry, Dad."

"I know, Son."

He patted me on the back and said, "Let's go inside and get a glass of sweet tea."

My dad turned to face Pallavi and her father. "Would you like to join us?"

"Yes, thank you," Pallavi's father replied. "My name is Sanjay Patel."

"Jeremy Paul," my dad said.

Pallavi and Mr. Patel walked along the fence and came around to our backyard. We all stepped on the back porch together. Pallavi and her father took off their shoes and lined them neatly on the porch.

"You don't have to do that," my dad said.

"We do this out of respect for your home," Mr. Patel said.

My dad opened the door. "Please, come in."

Mr. Patel and Pallavi walked through the house and directly into the kitchen. Dad grabbed a few glasses and the tea.

He gestured to the kitchen table. "Take a load off."

Pallavi and Mr. Patel looked at each other puzzled. "Take a load off?" he asked.

"Yep, it means you're welcome to sit," Dad replied.

They sat while Dad poured the tea.

Mr. Patel asked my dad, "What do you do?"

"I am a pharmacist."

"Was your father a pharmacist?" he asked.

"No, my dad worked at McClouth Steel," he said. "My pop had to work really hard to put me through school. I'm grateful every day."

He pointed to the books on the table. "Why do you have books about India?"

I chimed in. "I'm doing a report for school."

Pallavi said, "I could help, if you want."

"Thanks. I want to learn about Indian culture. I read one book today. It was interesting," I replied.

"If you want to learn about India, then you should start by actually talking to someone who's lived there," Pallavi's dad said.

"Do you mind if I interview you for my report?" I asked Pallavi.

"Pallavi, go with Brandon while Jeremy and I talk," he said.

I gathered my library books from the table and then led Pallavi into our living room. She sat on the chair and I sat on the couch.

"Okay, so my first question is, why did your father bow to my dad?" I asked.

"*Namaste* means hello, but it also is a sign of respect," she replied. "For example, if you were to greet my father, you would place your palms together, with your hands held in front of your chest, and then you would say, *Namaste*. Try it!"

I did as instructed.

Pallavi critiqued me. "Close, but this time do not look me in the eyes."

"Really? Because my dad always says that looking someone in the eyes shows honesty," I said.

"Well, in India to show respect, you do not look your elders in the eye while performing a respectful greeting," she stated. "Try again."

I placed my palms together, with my hands held in front of my chest. This time I did not maintain eye contact and said, "*Namaste.*"

Pallavi clapped. "You've got it!"

"Why did you take your shoes off before coming into the house?" I asked.

"Where I am from, the soles of your shoes are considered unclean and should never be pointed at anyone," she answered. "Removing our shoes showed your father that we respect him."

"So, if I did this," I brought my foot up to my knee and let the sole of the shoe face Pallavi, "it would be considered rude."

Pallavi got a sick look on her face. "Yes, very shameful."

I put my foot down, took off my shoes, and placed them by the door.

"Very good!" she said. "I have seen in movies

where a woman will threaten a man who is doing something shameful with her *chappal*—her sandal." Pallavi laughed.

"The man stole a *dosai*, a rice and lentil pancake, and the woman came from behind her stand to confront him with her sandal off," she said while smiling.

"What happened?" I asked.

"Oh, she did not have to use her sandal; he paid," Pallavi said. "You seem to enjoy flying kites. In Gujarat, kite flying is a tradition on January 14th. The sky during the International Kite Festival looks like one giant colorful mass swaying in the breeze. Some people even fight with kites."

I leaned in. "How do they do that?"

"Well, the goal is to entangle yourself with another kite and use your string as a makeshift knife," Pallavi explained. "Ultimately, the last kite flying is the winner. We have festivals and many kite fighters come from all over the world to compete. My father has done this before."

"Whoa. De'John and I are in a competition tomorrow," I said nervously. "I'm really worried that all my hard work will not pay off."

My dad and Mr. Patel walked into the living room.

"Did I hear that you're in a tournament?" Mr. Patel asked me.

"Yes, tomorrow I'll fly my kite at SeaWorld. Pallavi told me that you used to be a kite fighter."

He tilted his head sideways and raised his eyebrows

at me. I was very nervous and squirmed in my seat. Mr. Patel sat down next to me on the couch.

"I was a kite fighter. I spent much time looking at the sky. I was always kind to my opponent, until it came to snapping his line and collecting his kite."

He clapped his hands together and I worried that I was going to be snapped like a thin kite string.

"I have an idea! Let me show you a few tricks that will surely win you the competition tomorrow!" he shouted.

"Really? You would do that?" I asked.

Pallavi's dad grinned so big that it touched his eyes. "Yes, yes, of course. We are neighbors and that's what neighbors do for each other. Get your kite and meet me outside."

Pallavi, my dad, and Mr. Patel went outside while I ran to the garage to get the repaired kite.

Once outside, the lesson began.

"Okay, first you must make certain to wait for just the right gust of wind. You expend less energy if you are patient. Running with a kite over and over again, only to have it fall, is inefficient," Mr. Patel noted, as he placed the kite over his head. "Watch for the wings to lift simultaneously," he instructed.

We all watched as the wind tugged at the left wing and then the right, but never together.

"Don't worry, it will happen," Mr. Patel assured us. "Keep watching."

We waited as instructed.

"There, both wings are up!" I shouted.

Mr. Patel jogged only a few steps away and then let the kite gently lift into the air. You could see from his flawless liftoff that he was a pro.

"Can you show me a Yo-Fade?"

"Give me time to get some height."

I watched the kite getting smaller and smaller.

"Watch," he said in my direction.

Mr. Patel pulled the left string and the kite began to plummet toward the ground fast.

I immediately covered my eyes.

"Watch me, not the kite," he said sharply.

My hands slid down my face and I stood back so I could see his movements.

"This is it!" Mr. Patel took a few steps forward to offer slack on the line and then pumped both arms quickly and the kite rotated.

"Again!" he shouted and took a few steps forward to provide slack and the kite rotated.

While leveling the kite, he said, "Come over and try it for yourself."

"No, thank you."

My dad encouraged me. "Take the reins."

I walked over to Pallavi's dad where he handed me the controls, and suddenly I became the pilot.

"Just relax and let the kite climb."

I did as instructed, and Mr. Patel continued describing the trick.

"The key is to provide enough slack so your kite

can rotate. Some pilots fear the initial drop, but this is when you can thrill your audience. Let the kite plunge fast, and midway take a few long steps forward to lessen the tension. Then give two quick tugs on the line. Try it and see what happens."

The kite was high and hard to see, but I tugged on it so the nose would start to dive.

"Good, now wait," Mr. Patel whispered, as we watched the kite's descent.

"Now?" I shouted.

"Not yet!"

"I am going to pull up! My kite is going to crash!"

"Now, Brandon! Two long steps," he shouted.

I did as I was told and the kite's string was slack.

"Two quick pulls with both hands!"

I pulled back twice and the kite looped.

"Again!"

Two steps forward and two tugs later, I had made the kite do another Yo-Fade.

My dad whistled and Pallavi cheered.

"Okay, steady the kite and bring it down."

The kite leveled out and I slowly let it flutter to the ground.

As soon as the kite landed, I dropped the handles and punched the sky. "Yes, I did it!"

I stuck a hand out to offer Mr. Patel a handshake. He shook his head, placed his palms together under his chin, and said, "*Namaste.*" I smiled and did what Pallavi had taught me.

Smiling he said, "Tomorrow, I want to hear of a win."

"Thank you, sir. I won't forget your lessons."

Mr. Patel turned and walked toward his house. "Practice on your own and get a feel for your kite. Come, Pallavi. We will see Brandon tomorrow."

Before leaving, Pallavi took off her bracelet and began fiddling with the charms. She looked at me and said, "Open your hand. I've something for you."

I presented my hand palm up and a trinket appeared. The charm was strange. It was a small carving of a half-man, half-elephant creature.

"This is Ganesha, the mover of obstacles and the god of wisdom. Take him with you, and he will provide guidance and luck," she said.

"Thank you for Ganesha and for teaching me about your culture," I said.

Dad whispered in our direction, "Pallavi, your dad is ready to head home."

Pallavi turned and addressed my father. "Thank you, Mr. Paul, for the sweet tea."

My father and I walked Pallavi and Mr. Patel to the front yard.

"I hope you have enough information for your report and your competition," Pallavi's father said to me.

"Learned a lot today," I replied.

He nodded in agreement.

After Mr. Patel and Pallavi left, Dad and I went inside.

"Sanjay seems very nice. I might have been wrong about them. He invited us over for a traditional Hindi meal," my dad said to me.

I couldn't help grinning from ear to ear. I think the fire ignited more than just a spark—it lit a friendship.

Chapter 7

Small Pearls of Wisdom

"Brandon, are you ready?" Mom shouted from the kitchen.

I opened the door to my bedroom and poked my head out. "Be down in a minute."

Today was tournament day. De'John and I were going to compete at SeaWorld on Geauga Lake. This tournament would qualify us for the national championship, which would be held in San Diego, California. I tugged on both of the repaired wings. Satisfied that they were sturdy, I made my way down to the kitchen.

"Ready?" De'John asked.

I held up my kite. "Let the wind be our guide."

De'John lifted his kite in the air. "May the wind keep your wings and spirits afloat."

Keeping the kite above my head, I said, "Let's break wind!"

De'John let his kite fall to the ground and he doubled over laughing. "Let's break wind? That's a classic!"

"Oh, brother," I heard my mom say, as she ushered us out the front door.

In the driveway, De'John and I gently took our kites apart and placed everything strategically in the trunk.

After everyone was in the car, Mom turned to me and asked, "Got everything?"

"Yes," I replied.

She put the car in drive and turned on her favorite tunes.

After two bathroom breaks, one fast food joint, and three hours of Neil Diamond, we were finally pulling up to SeaWorld in Aurora, Ohio. As soon as my mother put the car in park, De'John and I jumped out. The trunk was popped and we quickly assembled our kites.

My mother locked the car and closed the trunk. She began plowing through her purse. "I have your wristbands here somewhere." She paused and looked up at me. "Did I give them to you?"

"No, but without them we won't be able to compete." I gave De'John a worried look.

"Okay, I know I have them here." She set her purse

on the closed trunk and began taking one item out at a time. De'John and I watched as tweezers, lipstick, loose change, a small screwdriver, tissue, a wallet, stamps, and a rock were pulled from the purse.

De'John whispered, "Wow, your mom carries everything."

I leaned in and whispered back, "We call it the black hole."

After a few tense minutes and lots of digging, she said, "Here they are. Put your wrists out." We did as we were told and Mom put on the bands.

De'John and I were excited and hurried to the park entrance with my mom. Our wristbands awarded us access to the park and the tournament. It was going to be a great day! We stepped in line, careful not to hit anyone with our large kite wings. The line was long and SeaWorld was crowded with families.

A tall man with a microphone stepped out from behind the ticket booth. "All tournament participants need to check their kites upon entering the park through the west entrance."

Anyone who had a kite began moving west toward a long registration table.

"Hey, over there." I pointed to the table and we followed the crowd.

A young girl in a bright shirt came by and stuck a numbered sticker on my kite.

"You can leave your kite here, and we'll give it to you right before the tournament." She then stuck another sticker on my chest. "This is your entry number. Do not lose it, and good luck!"

I looked down at my shirt and found the number thirteen; my kite had the same number.

"Hey, what number did you get?" De'John asked while admiring his sticker, which boasted twelve.

"Lucky number thirteen."

"Oh, man! Sorry, dude, that number is usually cursed."

"Not today. I have something special to counteract any bad luck." I put my hand in my left pocket and pulled out a small wooden elephant. "Pallavi gave me Ganesha, mover of obstacles and god of wisdom."

De'John lifted the object from my hand and closely inspected it. "Is that a man's body with an elephant's head attached?" he asked.

"Yes. Isn't it cool?" I replied.

"Hope it brings you good luck."

My mom stepped between us and unfolded a map with show times. "Okay, are we ready to take in a few shows before the tournament?" She pointed to the picture of Shamu. "Want to watch Shamu for Mayor? It looks like Shamu tosses his hat into the political ring!"

"De'John, what do you think?"

"Shamu's campaign sounds watered down if you ask me," he laughed.

I groaned. "Come on, Mr. Funny!"

Together we walked through the west entrance. A few feet in, my mom consulted the map and we headed toward Shamu Stadium. The show started and within a few minutes, we were soaked from head to toe. After watching Shamu, we went to a magic show starring The Great Sealini. A seal was the magician and his assistants were penguins. It was hilarious! We also journeyed through an amazing underwater shark tank and watched the playful macaroni penguins. Feeding the beluga whale was scary and being splashed by a bottlenose dolphin was fun! After the last show, my mom checked her watch.

"We've got to go! It's time for the tournament."

As we made our way past New Orleans Square, I shoved my hand in my pocket and found Ganesha. *Yep, still there.*

There were many patrons outside Water Ski Stadium where the tournament would be held.

A man wearing a SeaWorld shirt came from inside the stadium. "Doors will open in five minutes, folks."

A girl with blazing red hair turned around and directly faced me. She pointed to my number. "Are you in the tournament?"

"Sure am," I replied. "Lucky number thirteen."

"Did you hear that flying kites on this stretch of beach is dangerous? The beach front is small and so is the lake."

"Sounds like it will be hard to get altitude," I stated, grabbing De'John's arm to get his attention. He turned to face the wild-haired girl.

"Yep, and last year, kites were hitting the stadium

and one even sliced an audience member's arm," she said. She was silent, studying our faces. "Good luck out there, gentlemen."

The redheaded girl turned quickly and pushed her way to the front. We watched as she approached the SeaWorld employee. "I'm in the tournament, number twenty-two." The employee pointed to an obscure gray door. She parted from the crowd and slipped through.

Promptly I said to my mom, "De'John and I need to go get our kites."

She hugged both me and De'John. "Good luck. You'll find me in the front row, cheering you on."

We excused ourselves through the crowd and stood in front of the SeaWorld gatekeeper. "We're part of the tournament, numbers twelve and thirteen," I stated with confidence. Just as expected, he made a gesture toward the gray door.

De'John and I didn't need further explanation; we quickly scrambled to the gray entry. I grasped the handle, but De'John stopped me.

"I just wanted to say good luck, and I hope both of us place high enough to go to California."

"Ditto," I replied.

He moved out of the way, and I used my weight to pull open the heavy metal door. We were met with confusion, shouting, and kite flyers milling about. The holding area was tiny and crawling with people. I breathed deeply and smelled popcorn. I heard,

"Popcorn! Popcorn! Grab a fresh bag of popcorn!" and saw striped bags of goodness hanging from a long pole. A hand with money cut through the air. This alerted the popcorn attendant that a sale was about to be made. The nine-foot tree of striped bags and its handler made their way through the crowd using the dollar as a beacon.

"Is this what clowns feel like before they exit a car?" I shouted over the noise of the crowd.

De'John laughed. "Hang in there, buddy. We only have to be here for a bit."

Suddenly a voice was heard over the hustle and bustle. "Welcome, fellow kite enthusiasts." Eerie silence fell over the mass. De'John and I were pushed forward as the pack shifted their focus. Someone standing on a platform caught my attention.

I poked De'John. "Oh, my gosh. Is that who I think it is?"

"I can't believe it," he muttered.

The man on the platform began. "My name is Abhay Bindra." He clasped his hands together and bowed politely to the crowd. "*Namaste.* I am a five-time World Champion Master kite flyer, most recently flying in Berck-sur-Mer, France."

The crowd burst into applause. Abhay put his hand in the air to ask for silence.

"In Kolkata, kite flying is more than an occupation—it is a way of life. I have spent many hours looking up at a sky filled with radiant diamonds but am retiring from the game." He paused when the entire crowd gasped and begin to whisper among themselves. "I feel that it is important to encourage novice-level flyers, so today I am here as a judge. I wish you luck, but more important, I wish all of you a safe flying experience."

As Abhay finished his speech, flyer number one was ushered out of the door.

"Why can't we watch?" I asked De'John.

The redheaded girl turned around. "This competition will determine who will go to California, so only judges and the audience get to watch." She rolled her eyes. "Each contestant will be judged on control, timing, spacing, trick quality, complexity, technical difficulty, and landings. I plan to do a Coin Toss."

A SeaWorld employee announced, "Number two, please make your way down to the beach."

De'John turned to me and said, "Brandon, to win this thing we will both need to attempt a Yo-Fade."

The redheaded girl butted in again. "That's going to be tough. Really, only expert-level flyers can achieve that trick." She didn't wait for a response but instead whipped around and pushed through the crowd toward the exit.

"I don't know if I can do it. The last time I attempted it alone, my kite was smashed," I said to De'John. Mr. Patel wasn't here to guide me like he was last time.

"We have been working on backspin. Just extend the trick."

"Okay, let me think about it."

The door opened again and a SeaWorld employee called, "Number three, let's head down to the beach."

The feisty redhead stood near the door ready to pounce. "Hey, SeaWorld, how did numbers one and two do?"

The gentleman in the SeaWorld uniform replied, "The first flyer had a few nice moves. His Side Slide was amazing. Really clean lines. Number two had a wind shift and she lost her backspin, but I bet she still places high."

Flyer after flyer continued to be called, as I stood deep in thought going over my routine. The Yo-Fade was not in the plan, but it was obvious that I needed something to give me an edge. I must have lost track of time because suddenly I heard, "Number twelve, you're up."

De'John turned to me. "Wish me luck."

I patted him on the back. "You don't need luck when you've got talent."

He flashed a huge grin in my direction and then followed the SeaWorld employee.

The door shut and my hands started to sweat. Being on deck meant being very nervous. I felt like a grizzly in a sauna. I jammed my sweating hands into my pockets and found the charm Pallavi had given me. I flipped it over and over in my hand, memorizing the intricate details of the piece. The body looked similar to a man's but with a few extra arms, four to be exact. He was sitting with crossed legs next to what appeared to be a rat! A snake wrapped around one arm and his elephant head was adorned with a crown. After this was over, I would ask Pallavi what all these things symbolized. Suddenly the door swung open and I heard, "Number thirteen, you're up."

I placed the trinket back into my front pocket. "Here, I am here!"

"Great, follow me downstairs to the beach."

We began the descent down a long metal-encased staircase. The steps were cement and the walls were dimly lit. I stopped in my tracks after hearing clapping and cheering through the thin metal casing.

"The staircase runs along the entire pavilion; that's why you hear clapping," my guide commented.

"Wow, De'John must be doing really well."

"I hope better than the last person," the guide continued. "She lost control and the lake swallowed her kite whole."

We must have gone down a hundred stairs when a landing and a door finally emerged. Mr. SeaWorld used his shoulder to open the door and light blinded me. I used my hands as a makeshift shield to block the glaring sun. We were directly on a small narrow beach. The pavilion, which looked similar to large intricate bleachers, was on my left. I could have taken a sandy walk directly beneath the audience without anyone knowing. Mr. SeaWorld handed me something familiar—my kite!

"Follow me."

We rounded the pavilion and stood off to the side. I was unable to see De'John, but I could see his kite. He was currently performing a Fade. It was an easy trick but tough to do with precision.

"Yes, he nailed it!" I yelled while watching the kite soar over the water with accuracy.

Next, he maneuvered into a Side Slide to show the judges his control and speed. The kite horizontally panned over the water and rounded toward the audience. The spectators gasped as the kite flew inches from the pavilion. Thank goodness it didn't hit anyone. The last thing was a clean landing. As the kite floated to the ground like a feather, the audience clapped.

"Okay, go get 'em!" The SeaWorld attendant pointed toward the water while I clutched my kite and ran forward.

I heard my name over the loudspeaker. "Our next flyer comes from Flat Rock, Michigan. Brandon Paul, please begin when ready."

The crowd politely clapped. I lifted my kite above my head and began running toward the middle of the beach. It tugged away from my hand and I had liftoff. The first trick would be to show control, an Axel. The key is to stall the kite perfectly and then tug. As my kite began to stall, I moved forward to allow slack and then used my right hand to tug. The wings flattened out and rotated beautifully. The crowd gave a gentle clap. The next stunt would be a Fade. I just had to find the edge of a wind window. I felt the wind shift slightly, so I pulled both lines to steady the nose. I controlled the Fade by adjusting tension on the lines, and then just as the audience thought I was finished, I sailed right into a Side Slide. This time the crowd cheered. The last trick was supposed to be a Snap Stall, but the wind shifted again and I felt the kite tugging at my arms. I took a few steps forward, allowing for the kite to get some air and distance. I thought about Mr. Patel and his advice as the kite climbed higher and higher.

I could hear his advice in my mind: "Thrill your audience."

I pulled the kite into a vertical dive. The audience gasped, just like he said they would. As the kite came barreling back toward the water, I felt the wind shift again and saw the wings sputter in the air. If I did not do something fast, my kite would be lost in the lake. I quickly shuffled forward and then bent down on one knee, giving plenty of slack.

"Ouch!" Something was cutting into my leg. Without thinking, I pulled my left hand and the kite string to my leg. I felt the imprint of Ganesha's trunk. I looked up thinking I had just ruined the stunt but instead found the kite moving into a steady sideways position. Quickly I recovered and gave plenty of slack. Next I pulled quickly on both strings. To my delight, the kite rotated in the air! I then guided the kite back to the sand and the crowd went wild. I had done a Yo-Fade!

A woman with a Shamu T-shirt waved for me to leave the beach.

"The top ten contestants will compete in California," she instructed. "The list will be posted by the front entrance at two o'clock." I was then ushered to the front row of the pavilion, where I found a seat next to De'John.

He gave me a high-five. "Awesome!"

"Thanks, I really owe it to Pallavi's dad and Ganesha."

"How so?"

"I got some pointers from Mr. Patel and they really worked!"

"Well, how did Ganesha help you?"

"I knelt down and Ganesha poked me in the left leg, which caused me to move my arm toward the poke."

"So, you moved your left arm and the kite string because of Ganesha? That's creepy."

Someone ruffled my hair. "Great job, Brandon." My mom stood behind me. "I'm sure you both are going to place."

"California, here we come!"

She punched her fist above her head and shouted, "Let's break wind!"

The other contestants began laughing while I hid behind my kite.

"Good one, Mrs. Paul." De'John gave her a high-five.

"We have one hour before the results will be posted, so do you want to walk around and look at the shops?" my mom asked.

I peeked from behind my kite. "Yes, let's get out of here."

As we walked, my mom recounted our day. "What was your favorite part, De'John?"

"It was Shamu and competing in the tournament," he replied.

"What about you, Brandon?"

"My favorite part was performing the Yo-Fade, but I really owe that moment to Pallavi. If it were not for Ganesha poking me in the left leg, I would have never finished that trick."

The more I thought about it, the more I missed Pallavi and wished she could have been there to enjoy this special day.

De'John interrupted my thoughts. "Yuck, what is that smell?"

We were a few feet away from a souvenir shop that smelled fishy! The salesman running the shop shouted, "Live oysters! Pick a pearl!"

My mom stopped. "Did anyone want to try it?"

De'John pinched his nose. "No way!"

The shop owner came over and explained. "You stick your hand in this tank full of live oysters. Make sure to fish around a bit to get a good one. Then I pry open the shell and you get the pearl."

"Cool, let's try." I pulled out my wallet and

unleashed the Velcro. I had been saving my allowance for a new video game, but this was better. I paid the shop owner.

My mother asked the man for a few pointers when picking oysters and he said, "Pick the ugliest, hairiest, most disgusting oyster that you can find, because these produce the best pearls."

I dug around the smelly tank and pulled out a smooth white oyster, but the gentleman said it was much too pretty. I dropped the mollusk back into the water and tunneled deeper into the tank. After swishing around toward the bottom, I pulled out the most disgusting oyster that had ever been held by man. The bumpy shell was tinted gray and it looked hairy!

"Yep, that's the one!" the man said.

The shop owner took the horrendous oyster from my hand and dug a knife deep into the closed mouth of the mollusk. The lid popped open and unveiled a shiny white pearl.

He placed the oyster under my nose. "You will be the first human to ever touch this pearl. Pick it up."

I used my fingers as tweezers and gently lifted the pearl from its slimy nest.

"Now hold the pearl next to your heart and close your eyes," he instructed.

I did as I was told and then the gentleman said, "Now I want you to think of the most beautiful thing in the world because that will be this pearl's name."

Without skipping a beat, I replied, "Pallavi."

The shop owner smiled and said, "Pallavi is a beautiful name."

He gave me a wooden box from behind the counter. "This will ensure a safe journey home for your new pearl."

I opened the box and found it lined with soft white material. Placing the pearl inside, I said, "Thanks."

"Brandon, it's getting close to two o'clock," Mom reminded me.

I thanked the shop owner again, and we bolted to the front of the park only to be met by a huge crowd huddled around a large sheet of paper. The red-haired girl appeared next to us.

"Nice Yo-Fade," she said.

"Thanks," I replied.

"Did you look yet?" the girl asked.

"No, too many people."

"Well, don't wait...just push," she said.

As Miss Spitfire pushed angrily through the crowd, I turned to De'John and said, "Even if we don't place, I think we still won."

"We both worked hard and did our best," he replied.

De'John, my mom, and I waited patiently until the mob cleared a bit. Then we stepped forward and stood in front of the paper.

"Okay, let's see." I put my finger on the first number and began reading aloud, "Number nine, twelve, thirteen, twenty-five, and thirty-one!" De'John, my mom, and I started jumping for joy. We looked like we had just won the lottery.

De'John went back to the list and read it again. "I just can't believe it. We did it!"

"Great job, gentlemen." My mom gave both of us hugs. "Let's get home so we can share the news with your dad."

De'John and I had accomplished so much today. We had both worked very hard perfecting stunts and it paid off. We would be competing at the next competition.

"I can't wait to share the good news with Pallavi." I opened the box to sneak a peek at the pearl. I knew what I had to do to win Pallavi's heart and her father's permission.

After we dropped De'John off at home, I went directly to Pallavi's house. While walking past the hedges that separated the yards, I practiced my Hindi greeting. I had read it from a book and then asked Pallavi to pronounce it for me.

Aap kaise hai means, "How are you?" and right now, I was not good!

My nerves were getting the best of me. I was practically running, so I slowed down and took a deep breath. It did not seem to help. As I rounded the driveway and saw the front door, my stomach felt queasy. I pushed through the stomachache and walked up to the door. Before knocking, I opened the box once more and positioned the pearl so it would be presented in its best light. I placed the box gently in my coat pocket and knocked. Pallavi's father answered. I pressed my palms together, fixed my thumb to my forehead, and bowed deeply to show my respect.

I said, "*Namaste, aap kaise hai?*" and held my breath waiting for a reply.

Pallavi's father smiled and pressed his palms together, "*Namaste, tik hai.*"

I presented the small wooden box. "I would like to present your daughter with a gift." I opened the box to reveal the pearl.

"Come in, come in," Pallavi's father motioned for me to come into the house. I took my shoes off before entering and lined them up neatly next to the others. "Pallavi, you have a guest," he said.

She came down the stairs and stood in front of me.

I said, "Open your hand, please. I have a gift for you."

She did as instructed, and I placed the wooden box on her palm. She looked puzzled but opened the box. Her eyes lit up.

"A pearl is nature's most beautiful creation and so are you," I said. "I named the pearl Pallavi, in honor of your beauty inside and out."

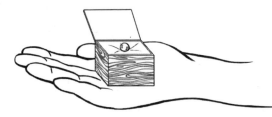

Pallavi was beaming from ear to ear. She

lifted the pearl from the box. Closing her hands around it, she said, "*Namaste,* I am honored by your gift."

"You are the gift," I replied. "Pallavi, you said that Ganesha would remove obstacles and provide wisdom, and he did."

Pallavi's mother poked her head out of the kitchen. "Brandon, I have been cooking all day. I am so excited to share a meal with you and your parents."

"Yes, when you come back you can tell us about the tournament," Pallavi said.

"Did you know that Pallavi's father was a kite fighter back in India?" her mother asked.

"Yes, I'm interested to hear about his wins," I said.

"Yes, hopefully we can share many meals and stories for years to come," Pallavi's mother said.

"Me, too!" Pallavi and I said in unison and then laughed.

Pallavi opened her palm again and the pearl rolled from side to side.

"Thank you, Pallavi, for helping me to understand your culture. At first I felt weird because things your family did and said were different. Now I can't wait to learn more about you."

"Sometimes I still feel that way, weird. The school cafeteria smelled strange and everyone was so loud," she replied.

"Is that why you ran out?" I asked.

"Yes, everything at this school is strange and I am

trying to fit in while keeping my family's traditions close."

"I can teach you and you can teach me. What do you think? This way you can keep your traditions but also learn about new things," I said.

She led me to the door. "I would like that."

"Me, too," I noted, as I stepped out onto the porch.

Pallavi gave a small wave before closing the door.

My heart skipped a beat.

Chapter 8

You've Got to Have Grit to Make a Pearl

"You look nice," my mother said, as I came down the stairs.

"Thanks," I replied, while fidgeting with my tie.

My mother and I walked into the kitchen where my father was busy packing squash soup.

My dad picked up the soup container. "I don't want to go empty-handed. Plus, what happens if I don't like what they serve," he stated.

I scratched my brown hair and thought about the next few words. "Dad, I don't think you should bring anything to the Patels'."

"Well, I heard Indian food was spicy and I might not like it."

My mother stepped between us. "Look, if you don't want to come, we'll understand. It's tough to try new stuff. No one is going to make you."

"Yeah, Dad, no one is going to twist your arm or anything," I chimed in.

"I just...," he stammered.

My mom shrugged and shook her head in disbelief. "Well, Sanjay just saved our shed, so I am going." She grabbed her jacket, which was hanging on the back of the kitchen chair, and turned to leave.

My dad caught her arm. "I want to go, but I'm nervous that I'll do something wrong. Do they use utensils? How will I understand what they are saying? As a family, will we be allowed to pray?"

My mother took the soup from between them and placed it on the table.

"Think about how the Patels feel. They are probably wondering if we will like their food or share in their customs."

"True."

"Come on, we've got a sitter for Melody, so let's try something new," she said.

My dad took my mom's hand and cradled it against his cheek.

"You're pretty amazing," he whispered.

"Ready?" I asked.

"Yes," my dad said. "I just need to grab the soup."

"What?!" my mom and I shouted.

"Just kidding," he laughed.

We used the sidewalk to find our way to the Patels' house. My dad knocked on the door and Mr. Patel opened it immediately.

"Welcome," Mr. Patel said, as he opened the door wide.

I stooped down to take my shoes off. Then I lined them up right next to another pair. My dad looked at me, puzzled. I motioned without Pallavi's dad noticing for my parents to take off their shoes. Finally, my mom's face registered understanding and she slipped off her high heels. My dad got the hint and did the same. He did not look happy after realizing that he had a hole in his sock.

"Just my luck," he whispered to me.

"No worries, you can barely see it," I whispered back.

My mom turned around and gave us the "you better stop whispering and behave" look.

Mr. Patel and my mom walked ahead into what appeared to be the living room.

She whipped back around to Mr. Patel and said, "So glad you asked us to dinner."

Mrs. Patel emerged from the kitchen.

Mr. Patel began the introductions. "This is my wife, Haleema."

"It's nice to meet you," Mrs. Patel replied.

"Haleema, this is my wife, Carol, and you have already met my son, Brandon," my dad said while trying to cover up his sock hole.

My mother walked across the room and jutted her hand out in Mrs. Patel's direction. She smiled and shook my mother's hand. She then placed her palms together under her chin, bowed, and said, "*Namaste.*"

My mother then awkwardly placed her hands together, bowed, and said, "*Namaste.*"

"*Namaste* literally means, I bow to you, but it also means much more. I have respect for you, I recognize that we are all equal, are just a few interpretations," Mrs. Patel said with a smile. She gestured toward the kitchen. "Come, Pallavi is in the kitchen."

The Patels' kitchen was enormous. One entire wall was stacked with floor-to-ceiling cabinets. The countertops were squeaky clean and the stovetop was stationed inside an island. A large maple table was to our right, and to our left was another opening that led to a mudroom and the porch door.

"Haleema, you have a beautiful kitchen," my mother said.

"Thank you. Tonight we are going to eat around the kitchen island so you can see how the meal is being prepared," Haleema said, as she opened a lid on the stove and began to stir. Everyone sat on a large stool, watching Pallavi move about the kitchen. "First we are going to make *poori*, Indian fry bread. I would beg my aunt to make this bread every time we went to her house."

Mrs. Patel went to the refrigerator and took out

a covered dish. "I made this dough earlier. Brandon, would you like to cut and roll?"

"Sure, I think I can handle that," I replied.

Pallavi opened a container with flour and sprinkled it on the counter in front of me. She then handed me a tiny rolling pin.

Mrs. Patel took the dough out of the bowl and slapped it on the countertop in front of me.

"Okay, rip the dough into six equal pieces," Pallavi instructed.

I did as I was told.

"Now use the small rolling pin to flatten out the dough. You need it to be about ¼-inch thick."

Mr. Patel put a large pan on the stove and then poured a good amount of oil in it to heat.

There were no handles on the sides of the rolling pin. I fumbled around trying to use both hands on the roller. Pallavi took it from my hands. "Roll like this."

She only used one hand to manipulate the roller back and forth. The bread took shape and quickly flattened.

"Now you try," she said while handing me the small tool.

I tried to mimic Pallavi by using my palm to move the roller back and forth. The dough slipped away and the roller was hard to control.

"Wow, this is really hard to do. You make it look easy, Pallavi," I said.

Pallavi took pity on me. "No, you are doing well

for your first time. I think that piece of dough looks about right."

I raised the roller so she could hand the flattened, flimsy dough to her father. He then gently laid it in the oil. You could hear the oil popping and protesting.

"Let me try, Brandon," my dad said.

I slid over and gave him the small rolling pin. He laid the dough in front of himself and used one hand to roll it flat.

"Hey, I am pretty good at this!" he exclaimed.

Pallavi's dad flipped the fried bread in the pan. "I am almost ready for another one," he said.

A few minutes later, my dad had flattened all of the dough and began handing them to Mr. Patel to cook like an assembly line. Each bread only fried for about three minutes.

"Ready to eat?" Mr. Patel asked after most of the bread had been fried.

"Yes, please," I replied.

Pallavi went to the refrigerator and brought a small bowl to the kitchen island.

Sanjay took fried bread and tore a small piece off.

"First you rip the bread and then you dip it into the

chutney dipping sauce," he explained.

I ripped and then dipped. The bread was puffy. The sauce was amazing and full of flavor.

"What is this sauce?" I asked.

"Chutney is a mixture of black peppercorns, cloves, cinnamon, cumin seeds, and cardamom pods. We usually roast and grind our own spice mixtures," Pallavi replied.

"There's a lot I don't know about cooking," my mom said. She tore another piece of bread and dipped into the chutney again. "I wish I knew how to cook like this!"

"Pallavi and I can teach you," said Mrs. Patel. "We are new to Flat Rock and I could use some help finding the library, movie theaters, and best places to buy produce. Do you think if I helped you that you might help Pallavi and me?"

My mother looked delighted and replied, "Yes, of course! I would love to! That's what neighbors are for."

"A few days ago you gave me *naan* bread. Could you show me and my mom how to make it?" I asked Pallavi.

"Yes, it's easy. For *naan* bread, you only need a few ingredients."

"Don't forget the hot plate," Mrs. Patel reminded.

"Oh, yeah, that really makes a difference," Pallavi commented.

"This sounds complicated," I said.

"Well, my grandmother showed me a few shortcuts."

Mr. Patel interrupted. "Okay, so who here likes a lot of spice?"

My dad's hand shot up into the air. "Bring it on, Sanjay!"

Mr. Patel laughed. "Well, my wife makes the sauce, but I add the spice to the Kadai Chicken. Ghee enhances the flavor, but I suppose the red and green chilies give the dish some zing! I don't really think it is that spicy, but some of my friends at the university ran for water after one bite."

We all started laughing, including my dad. He was starting to loosen up and have a good time. He seemed to have forgotten all about his holey sock and nervousness.

Pallavi smiled at me and I gave a shy grin back. As Mr. Patel threw some seeds and nuts in a pan to roast, I realized that our families were just like that. Let's face it, my family were the nuts and the Patels were the seeds. Apart, we really did nothing to a dish, but together, we could really add some zing! Our time together was not about tolerance but about learning and understanding. I had a feeling that tonight was going to be just the beginning of many family dinners with the Patels. Well…I hoped.

Chapter 9

Cultured Pearls

-*Current Time*-

Moti was struggling not to fall asleep. Brandon paused in the telling of his story to look at his daughter. She had her mother's silky black hair and beautiful brown eyes. He smiled, remembering the day Pallavi had become his neighbor. At first both families had been unwilling to accept each other's differences. Eventually shared meals and conversation had revealed things they had in common and a deep friendship had developed.

"Is that when you and Mom fell in love?" she asked. "When you gave her the pearl?"

Brandon tucked the blanket under Moti's chin.

"Oysters produce lovely gifts but not overnight," he replied. "They need time, the right conditions, and enough grit to make a pearl. Love is similar. If given time, the right conditions, and grit, eventually friendship can transform into something new."

The door creaked and Pallavi poked her head into the room.

"I just came to kiss my little pearl goodnight," she said.

"Mommy, Daddy told me the story about when you met."

Pallavi opened the door further and looked at Brandon. "Oh, did he?" she asked, as she winked.

Brandon extended his clenched hand toward Pallavi.

She walked into the room and put her hand out to receive Brandon's gift. "What's this?" she asked.

"A pearl is nature's most beautiful creation and so are you," he said. "I named the pearl, Pallavi, in honor of your beauty inside and out."

Brandon dropped the pearl into her hand.

Pallavi took the necklace and placed it close to her heart. Brandon studied her face, as she struggled to make a decision. She took one last look at her cherished pearl and then gently set the necklace on Moti's nightstand.

"I'm glad our families learned to love each other despite our differences. If not, we would have missed out on our little pearl." She reached out and smoothed her daughter's hair, then took Brandon's hand.

Lowering her voice, she said, "Our sleeping little girl," and motioned toward the door.

Pallavi stood up and led Brandon out of the room, but before closing Moti's door, she took one last look at the tiny pearl and smiled.

Cool Facts

Here are some cool facts about where Pallavi's family comes from:

State: Gujarat
Country: India
District: Vadodara, the third largest city in the Indian State of Gujarat.
Population: Total 2,065,771 (1.2 billion for the country)
Official Languages: Gujarati, Marathi, Hindi, and English
Largest City: Ahmedabad in Gujarat
Climate: Tropical savanna
Two Major Religions: Hinduism and Islam

Traditional Indian Food: Fish, chicken, rice, breads; many spices are used

Traditional Indian Women's Clothing: Due to their customs, traditions, and religion, women all over India wear saris, which are made of cotton or silk, wrapped around the body, and are usually five to seven feet long. Women and men decorate their foreheads with bindi, or dots, in either red or black, that vary in size and shape depending upon the occasion. Temporary henna tattoos are used to decorate women's hands, feet, and other parts of the body for various special occasions.

Production: Tea, rice, and grain are the three major crops.

Government: India is a democracy. It has a president who is in charge of the state and a prime minister as head of government. States were created based on history, culture, and language.

Celebrations: Each temple celebrates its own festivals. The following are traditional Hindu festivals and holidays that are celebrated in different parts of India. These common festivals are based on the Indian lunar calendar. The dates listed can vary from year to year and this list does not include all festivities.

January–February (Magha)

Vasant Panchami is a spring festival. This is a one-day celebration that honors Saraswati, the goddess of learning. Traditionally people wear yellow, fly kites, and bless schoolchildren's materials.

February–March (Phalguna)

Holi is a water festival that celebrates the coming of spring. It begins during a full moon. On the first night a huge bonfire is lit to roast grains. The next day people take to the streets to throw paint, colored water, and colored powder.

March–April (Chaitra)

Cheti Chand is celebrated in honor of the lunar new year. This is celebrated primarily in South India.

April–May

Baisakhi to Hindus is the solar new year. Dancing and singing mark this celebration.

July–August (Shravana)

Independence Day is celebrated to mark the anniversary of India's independence from Britain.

October–November (Kartika)
Diwali or Deepavali is the Festival of lights. Firecrackers, lighting oil lamps, and giving sweet gifts are used to celebrate Rama and Sita's homecoming in the Ramayana.

Sources:
Thomas, Gavin. *The Rough Guide to Rajasthan, Dehli & Agra.* (United States: Rough Guides, 2010), 7, 9-10, 53-55, 401-403.

Nicholson, Louise. *National Geographic Traveler India.* (Washington D.C.: National Geographic, 2007), 16, 19, 244-245, 326.

"How Indian Tradition Works,"
http://people.howstuffworks.com/culture-traditions/national-traditions/indian-tradition1.htm.

Dear Reader,

Have you ever wanted to be friends with someone from a different culture but felt weird about it? Well, many teens find themselves questioning how to overcome social pressures related to diversity. Tomorrow at school, consider opening up and making a new friend. Speak up in class and let people know about your own beliefs, values, and customs. Please encourage others to do the same. Below you will find three quick tips for developing a diverse friend portfolio:

• Join a club that you would not normally consider. Many times brilliant people are hiding in the most obvious places.

• Try being open-minded at lunchtime. Often we sit at the same table day after day. If everyone simply moved seats for one day, they might find a new friend.

• If there is someone from another culture with whom you'd like to chat, consider doing some research first. Find out about their customs and first language. They will be flattered that you took the time to gather more information about them.

Diversity is something to be celebrated and, by reading this book, you are part of the party! A portion of the proceeds will be used to purchase books with diverse main characters for local schools. By purchasing this book, you have voted for diversity! Thank you!

I would love to hear about your experiences with diversity. Please feel free to email me at capaulo813@gmail.com. I look forward to responding to your emails.

Your Friend,

Carol Paul

Let's Start a Book Club!

Today is a great day to start a book club. It is easy to start; all you need is an interesting book and a few guiding questions. Below you will find some helpful tips to help you get started.

- Pick an interesting book that you and other members will enjoy.
- A book club is a big commitment! Make certain to read your book each and every day. You can read the book together in a circle or you can assign pages to be read at home.
- Talk about what you have read. Discuss your thoughts, feelings, or pivotal parts of the book. These are great

ways to expand understanding. Make sure everyone gets a chance to talk and please be courteous.
• Use thought-provoking questions to spice up your book club. Below you will find questions to help you get started in creating a book club for *Breaking Wind*.

Breaking Wind Book Club Questions

Chapter 1: Come Out, Come Out, Wherever You Are!

• When does Chapter 1 take place?
• Describe what happens when Brandon can't find Moti.
• Why do you think Moti is interested in the pearl necklace?
• What does the name Moti mean?
• Who is Daisy and what impact does she have on the beginning of the story?

Chapter 2: Wishes Are Kooky

• How old is Brandon in Chapter 2?
• Describe a few birthday traditions that Brandon's family has.
• Describe any traditions that your family celebrates.

- After blowing out the candles, what does Brandon wish for?
- Devise a plan as to how you would get the kite back.
- How are the birthday wish and the new girl next door linked?

Chapter 3: Pain in the Neck

- Why do you think Brandon keeps thinking about the girl next door?
- Brandon tries naan, a customary Indian bread, for the first time. What new things have you tried lately?
- Locate Gujarat on the map. What sea does Gujarat border?

Chapter 4: This Puppy Is Barking Up the Wrong Tree

- In Chapter 4, what problem do Brandon and De'John encounter?
- Why do you think Principal Cole vouches for Brandon's character?
- If a principal, teacher, or classmate had to describe your character, what do you think they would say? Explain.
- Go online and watch someone playing the sitar. Describe what it sounds like to you.
- Mrs. Patel states, "Stay away from that boy. I saw

him at Hobby Hill today." Why would she not want Brandon and Pallavi to be friends?

Chapter 5: Soaring Through Differences

- Why is this chapter titled, "Soaring Through Differences"?
- Think about Brandon's dream. What does it mean?
- On Pallavi's first day in an American school, what might she fear?
- Do you remember your first day of school? If so, describe how you felt.
- Infer why Pallavi left the lunchroom.
- Why do you think Brandon is nervous about knocking on Pallavi's front door?
- What caused Brandon to knock on Pallavi's door? What was the effect?
- Why would Brandon want to learn more about his neighbors even after his dad said to stay away from them?

Chapter 6: Igniting a New Friendship

- What motivated Brandon to read about India?
- What was the cause of the fire? How did the fire

affect the relationship between the Pauls and the Patels?
- What do the words "namaste" and "chappal" mean? Use the text and context clues.
- What do Brandon and Mr. Patel have in common? How does this change their relationship?
- Summarize what Brandon has learned so far about the Indian culture.

Chapter 7: Small Pearls of Wisdom

- Why is Brandon nervous about the tournament?
- How does Pallavi help Brandon during the tournament?
- What can you infer from Brandon naming the pearl after Pallavi?
- Brandon behaves differently the second time he visits Pallavi's house. Describe these differences.
- In this chapter we learn why Pallavi left the cafeteria. Was this different than what you inferred? How did it compare?
- Pallavi states the following, "Yes, everything at this school is strange and I am trying to fit in while keeping my family's traditions close." Why do you think this is important to Pallavi? Are traditions important to your family?

Chapter 8: You've Got to Have Grit to Make a Pearl

- How does Brandon's dad change throughout the story?
- Summarize the major differences between Indian and American culture.
- How did Brandon change throughout the story? What did he learn?

Chapter 9: Cultured Pearls

- Read the following quote: "Oysters produce lovely gifts but not overnight. They need time, the right conditions, and enough grit to make a pearl. Love is similar. If given time, the right conditions, and grit, eventually friendship can transform into something new." What is Brandon comparing? What is he trying to tell Moti?
- Why do you think Pallavi struggled to give the pearl to her daughter?
- How was the pearl connected to Brandon, Pallavi, and Moti?
- Why did the author write this story?
- What was the author's main message?

About the Author
Carol Paul

The Michigan Reading Association has described Carol Paul as a fierce advocate for literacy in sheep's skin. In 2010, the MRA awarded Carol the Adult Literacy Grant for her work at Henry Ford Community College. The association recognized her again in 2014 as a leader with the Individual Literacy Award. Mrs. Paul is a lifelong learner, which is evident from her collegiate career, graduating from Eastern Michigan University, University of Michigan-Dearborn, and Wayne State. Majoring in Elementary Science, Reading, and English Learners, Carol understands current educational issues and is not afraid to speak up. She currently serves as the State and Federal Programs Coordinator for the Summit Academy North and Summit Academy school district. She has taught at a variety of grade levels from elementary to college while staying active in the Michigan Reading Association, Michigan Council on Literacy for Adults, and the Wayne County Reading Council. When she is not working with students and staff at her school, Carol is presenting at local conferences within the state of Michigan. Carol has stated, "The field of literacy has much to offer, and I am honored to be a part of it. Although any discipline is going to come with challenges, I believe these tests will make us all stronger literacy leaders."

Mrs. Paul currently lives in Flat Rock, Michigan, with her loving husband, Jeremy, her computer enthusiast son, Brandon, her talented daughter, Melody, and a cute Springer Spaniel named Dottie. She enjoys reading and writing, and is an avid literacy activist and presenter.

About the Illustrator
Corryn Hoen

Growing up in Livonia, Michigan, Corryn Hoen always loved art, but she didn't realize she'd make it her career. She earned her BFA in Illustration with a minor in Digital Media from Kendall College of Art and Design. There she learned of her two loves: watercolor painting and pressing "Command-Z." When she's not working, Corryn enjoys reading, watching thunderstorms, and knitting lots of beards. One day she'll put them on Etsy. One day...